Olivia & Connor!
Get out
& Play in the
Dirt!

Hayley

This awesome book belongs to

**Thank you to my ever expanding GeEK Team.
You all make every journey amazing!**

CIP Data
Name: Taylor, Lori Author/Illustrator
Title: Holly Wild: The Young GeEK's Guide to Getting Outside
Description: Pinckney, MI : Bear Track Press, 2015
Summary: Ten-year old Holly Wild and friends entertain young
cousins for the day by taking them on an outdoor alphabet adventure.
Identifiers: 1st U.S. Edition | (hardcover) | First Printing, Oct. 2015
Subjects: CYAC: Stories in rhyme. |Alphabet—fiction.
| Backyard—fiction. | Nature—fiction. | Imagination—fiction.
ISBN 978-0-692-47848-6
LCCN: pending (print)

Published in the U.S.A., Oct. 2015
by Bear Track Press, Pinckney, MI
Signature Book Printing, www.sbpbooks.com
Printed in the U.S.A.

www.loritaylorart.com

We love you Mr. Pickles

For
Kyah and Mae!
Play in the dirt
---always!
♥ Gram

Wake your inner squatch.

A for adventure, let's get up and go!

B is for backpack, for gear that we stow.

B

C is for camping, by the creek is the best.

D for directions, north, south, east, and west.

Never ask a squirrel for directions!

Follow directions when outdoors, and use the GeEK "Buddy System." Practice and HOLD your BUDDY'S hand UP HIGH!

E is for earth, we dig up and explore.

EWW!

EEK!

FIND and point to the ITEMS the kids think they found:

elephant bone
Egyptian eyeglasses
evil eyes three

earthworm
eagle claw fossil
early explorer footwear

F is for friends, take one or take four!

G for granola, a tasty GeEK snack!

Gorp Recipe!
M&Ms
raisins
nuts
Add granola or dry cereal. Toss in zip-locking bag for a super, sweet snack!

H is for hiking, wear socks, shoes, and hat.

I is for ivy on that tree trunk!

Practice this RHYME out loud!

"Leaves of Three LET IT BE!"

Poison Ivy

* Droopy three-leafed plant can CLING to trees with its "HAIRY-LEG" vines and also grows close to the ground.

J is for jars to hold cool stuff and junk.

SAND

* Enjoy, thank, and RELEASE all livings things, please!

13

K is for kayak, a small boat for one.

Holly Kayaking

* Paddle YOUR "kayak" DOWN a stream!

14

L is for listen, making deer ears is fun.

Make DEER ears. Cup your hands behind your EARS to hear better. Make the SOUNDS of things you see on these pages.

M is for map, showing lakes, trails, and trees.

N is for nose, to smell clues on the breeze.

* Moths and butterflies smell with their FEET or ANTENNAE! Make a butterfly with your HANDS, thumbs crossed. FLAP and wiggle your THUMB antennae as you describe SMELLS in the picture.

O is for owl eyes, we sit still and look.

* Make OWL eye "binoculars" with your hands. Now count how many EYES are watching YOU?

P is for pencil, to draw in a sketchbook.

Scientists DRAW and WRITE "field notes" telling the story of their day. Be a scientist, name the SEASON, WEATHER in this picture. Name the LIVING THINGS you see here.

Q is for quiet, to see more on your quest.

* How QUIETLY can you CLAP your HANDS?

R is for rocks, choose one, leave the rest.

S is for sign, like snakeskin and scat.

* "SIGN," like scat (poo), food items, and tracks is an animal's "STICKY NOTE" that says, "I was here!" How many can you find?

T is for trail, tracks go this way and that.

Match the animal TRACKS to its trail and "track-maker"!

23

U for up and under, where we find nature clues.

V is for vest, to hold tools that you use.

* What other TOOLS would you carry? PULL it out of your POCKET!

W is for world, GeEKs help keep it neat.

X marks the treasure found at your feet.

Y is for yowling like Yetis when we play!

Z is for Z-Z-Zs, a nap ending the day.

Now I know GeEK ABCs,
Let's go look for more than these!

CAMP SKWATChA GeEK

the end

IT'S A JUNGLE OUT THERE!

HAVE FUN!
BE SAFE!
BE AWARE!

BUNNY ears,
RED leaves in FALL,
Touch NOT this
Wetland SHRUB
AT ALL!

POISON SUMAC

PLANTS TO
WATCH OUT
FOR!

TALL and SPIKY,
Umbrella-topped,
With PURPLE stem,
Means DANGER!
STOP!

GIANT HOGWEED

STOP

HOLLY WILD GEEK CLUB!

(Geo-Explorer Kid)

Mae

Max

Karen and Hershey

CONGRATULATIONS! YOU ARE NOW A GEEK!

Look at these pictures. Make the SOUNDS you think you might hear. What do you think these things would FEEL like?

Jenna

Your backyard is filled with hidden secrets! Get out and find them. Walk TALL and slow. LOOK and LISTEN. SMELL and TOUCH.

Kenny

DIGGING CAMP

Shields

Cooper and Emma

LOOK at the pages for one minute, then CLOSE your eyes. How many INSECTS do you remember? How many BOTTLES? ANIMALS?

33

WILD OUTSIDE: BACKYARD CORNER!

- **Snakes ROCK**—Pile up rocks for snakes to warm their snakey bodies and bones!

- **Wild Toad Abode**—Lay broken clay pots on their side for toads to hide.

- **Wild GeEK Art**—Arrange, stack, and build "found" things (pots, dishes, relics, etc.) and natural bits (logs, sticks, stumps, etc.) to make your sitting place special.

- **Wild GeEK Garden**—Plant for bees, butterflies, and birds! Tall grasses in back, short plants in front. Sunflowers and milkweed are tall favorites of butterflies and birds. Plant native plants in your *corner* and place other plants in pots or cement blocks! **Then sit and watch** to see who visits your Wild Corner!

Always get permission first!

BOOK HIDE-N-SEEK

Sharpen your eyes! Look for the object on the page with the **alphabet letter.** Use the alphabet letter to spell out a mysterious word!

Answer on back page.

MY BACKYARD BINGO!

Squatch Fact: *A habitat is a place where animals live. It gives birds, insects, mammals, and others a place to rest, nest, eat, and drink. Write and draw your discoveries while you play!*

BIRDS	INSECTS	NESTS	GROWERS	OTHERS
perched	sound	bug home	poky plant	mammal
bright color	flying	bird nest	seeds	cold-blooded critter
flying	crawling	FREE SPACE	tiny plants	scat
singing	hiding	web	smell	animal food item
dull color	larva	ground home	leafy noise	animal track

Gather Pebble markers. Lay the book flat. Cover space with a Pebble after finding each thing. Get FIVE in a row, shout BINGO!

GET OUTSIDE FOR SCAVENGER HUNT BINGO AND GET TO KNOW YOUR BACKYARD!

GET WILD!

Growing up in Clarkston, Michigan, I often kept a small survival kit in my pocket. Fish hooks, line, safety pins, zip locking bags—and **always** paper and pen. As kids we spent our days in the "back forty" splashing for tadpoles, climbing apple trees, digging for treasure, biking wooded trails, building forts, and reading under pines with a PBJ.

Later, my own kids picnicked in nearby woods, combed cornfields for wild strawberries and artifacts, and slept out in tents. Now I camp with grandchildren and build fairy houses in my backyard. Kids don't need to go far for adventure! Just get out and play wild.

"There's more to explore out there!"

Lori Taylor is the author/illustrator of the HOLLY WILD nature mystery series, along with several other mid-grade fiction titles. Lori is a freelance illustrator and works for Bear Track Press in Pinckney, MI. She was artist-in-residence for Sleeping Bear Dunes National Lakeshore and Porcupine Mountains Wilderness State Park. When she is not making books, she hikes, bikes, and kayaks wild places for story.

MORE BOOKS FROM BEAR TRACK PRESS

HOLLY WILD:
Bamboozled on Beaver Island (Bk. 1)
Let Sleeping Bear Dunes Lie (Bk. 2)
Packing for the Porkies (Bk. 3)
Questpedition for da Yooper Stone (Bk. 4)
HOLLY WILD: Sketch-n-Color Book

LISSY-LOST!
CRAZY CAT: Don't Chase That Rabbit!
HOT TIMES In the Big Creek Wood

BEAR TRACK PRESS

Hide-n-Seek answer: Skwatch

WWW.LORITAYLORART.COM